Gets it Wrong

by Elizabeth Dale and Maxine Lee

Robbie the robot
lived with the Browns.
He had lots of jobs.
He made the beds
and cleaned the house.

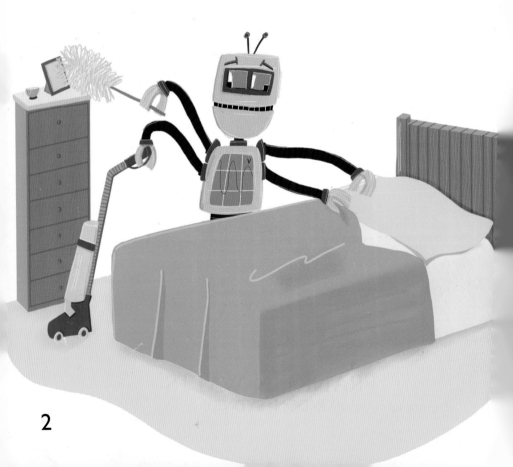

He put the washing on the line.

He dug the garden, too.

Robbie liked to help.

One day, Robbie did not help.

"Turn off the hose, please,"
said Mrs Brown.

But Robbie did not turn off the hose.

The water went on Mr and Mrs Brown.

"Stop it, Robbie!" said Mrs Brown.

"I am wet," said Mrs Brown.

"And I am cold," said Mr Brown.

"Get us a drink

to warm us up, please."

But Robbie did not get
something hot.
He got something cold!

Robbie got lots and lots
and LOTS of ice cream.

Mrs Brown was cross.

"No!" she said. "Stop it, Robbie!

Clean up this mess, please."

But Robbie did not clean up.

He made more and more mess.

"Stop it, Robbie!" said Mrs Brown.

"Please stop it!"

But Robbie did not stop it.

Mrs Brown went to help Robbie

but she slipped on the ice cream.

"Oh dear!" she said.

"Robbie is broken.

He will have to be fixed."

13

Mrs Brown took Robbie

back to the robot shop.

"Can you fix him, please?" she said.

The man looked at Robbie.

"It will be a big job," he said.

Robbie was at the shop

for weeks and weeks.

When he came back,

he looked just like new.

"Make me a cup of tea, please,"

said Mrs Brown.

Robbie wanted to help.

He went into the kitchen.

He came back with ice cream ...

... and a cup of tea for Mrs Brown.

"Hurray!" everyone said.

"Robbie the robot is fixed."

Robbie just smiled.

He liked to help.

Story order

Look at these 5 pictures and captions.
Put the pictures in the right order
to retell the story.

1

Robbie got a cup of tea for Mrs Brown.

2

Robbie went to be fixed.

3

Robbie got too much ice cream.

4

Robbie did lots of jobs at home.

5

Mr and Mrs Brown got wet.

Independent Reading

This series is designed to provide an opportunity for your child to read on their own. These notes are written for you to help your child choose a book and to read it independently.

In school, your child's teacher will often be using reading books which have been banded to support the process of learning to read. Use the book band colour your child is reading in school to help you make a good choice. *Robot Gets It Wrong* is a good choice for children reading at Orange Band in their classroom to read independently.

The aim of independent reading is to read this book with ease, so that your child enjoys the story and relates it to their own experiences.

About the book

Robbie the robot is always very helpful. He does lots of jobs. But one day, Robbie starts doing everything wrong, so he goes off to be fixed. When he comes back, the Browns aren't sure if he is fixed or not. He still wants to fetch the children ice cream, and where is Mrs Brown's cup of tea?

Before reading

Help your child to learn how to make good choices by asking: "Why did you choose this book? Why do you think you will enjoy it?" Look at the cover together and ask: "What do you think the story will be about?" Ask your child to think of what they already know about the story context. Then ask your child to read the title aloud.

Ask: "What do you know about robots? Do they usually help people?" Remind your child that they can sound out the letters to make a word if they get stuck.

Decide together whether your child will read the story independently or read it aloud to you.

During reading

Remind your child of what they know and what they can do independently. If reading aloud, support your child if they hesitate or ask for help by telling the word. If reading to themselves, remind your child that they can come and ask for your help if stuck.

After reading

Support comprehension by asking your child to tell you about the story. Use the story order puzzle to encourage your child to retell the story in the right sequence, in their own words. The correct sequence can be found on the next page.

Help your child think about the messages in the book that go beyond the story and ask: "Would you like to have a robot to help you in your home? Why/why not?"

Give your child a chance to respond to the story: "Did you have a favourite part? Which job would you most like a robot to do for you at home?"

Extending learning

Help your child understand the story structure by using the same sentence patterning and adding different elements. "Let's make up a new story about a robot going wrong. Where does this robot live? What jobs does it do? How will it go wrong?"

In the classroom, your child's teacher may be teaching how to use speech marks to show when characters are speaking.

There are many examples in this book that you could look at with your child. Find these together and point out how the end punctuation (comma, full stop, exclamation mark or question mark) comes inside the speech mark.

Franklin Watts
First published in Great Britain in 2017
by The Watts Publishing Group

Copyright © The Watts Publishing Group 2017

Series Editors: Jackie Hamley and Melanie Palmer
Series Advisors: Dr Sue Bodman and Glen Franklin
Series Designer: Peter Scoulding

A CIP catalogue record for this book is
available from the British Library.

ISBN 978 1 4451 5425 1 (hbk)
ISBN 978 1 4451 5426 8 (pbk)
ISBN 978 1 4451 6102 0 (library ebook)

Printed in China

Franklin Watts
An imprint of
Hachette Children's Group
Part of The Watts Publishing Group
Carmelite House
50 Victoria Embankment
London EC4Y 0DZ

An Hachette UK Company
www.hachette.co.uk

www.franklinwatts.co.uk

FSC
www.fsc.org
MIX
Paper from
responsible sources
FSC® C104740

Answer to Story order: 4, 5, 3, 2, 1